The Robins Knew

written by Carolyn Koster Yost

illustrated by Katherine W. Gardner

"With your wisdom you made them all."-Psalm 104:24

Library of Congress Catalog Card Number 90-72098
© 1991, The STANDARD PUBLISHING Company, Cincinnati, Ohio
Division of STANDEX INTERNATIONAL Corporeation. Printed in U.S.A.

Father and Mother Robin flew up o
the porch of Kimberly's house, flappit
flap, flappity-flap.

God knew why, and the robins knew why. Do you know why?

From the window, Kimberly saw
Father Robin cock his head as he looke
at a place just under the roof. Mother
Robin blinked one eye to say she liked
that spot.

Then the robins flew off, flappity-fla
flappity-flap.

Soon the birds were back with straw in their beaks. Back and forth, back and forth the robins flew with bits of straw and dried grass. Their wings went flappity-flap, flappity-flap.

They tucked the straw and grass into a round shape, tuckity-tuck, tuckity-tuck.

God knew why, and the robins knew why. Do you know why?

Then the robins brought dabs of mud
to the nest and pushed the mud around
the straw. Mother Robin sat in the straw
and mud and turned round and round
while Father Robin watched.

Then the birds flew off again,
flappity-flap, flappity-flap.

Before long, Mother Robin began sitting on the nest every day. She sat quietly, so quietly. She only blinked her eyes, blinkity-blink, blinkity-blink.

Father Robin stayed nearby in the trees or in the yard. Kimberly wanted see the nest up close, but Father Robin warned her away. "Cheat, cheat, cheat he screamed.

God knew why, and the robins knew why. Do you know why?

So Kimberly watched from the window.

One day Kimberly saw Mother Robin fly to the nest with a worm in her beak. A tiny, bald head poked up and took the worm. Then Father Robin came with a worm in his beak, and another little head bobbed up with its mouth open. Then yet another bobbed up.

"There are baby birds in there!"
Kimberly said in surprise.
    Back and forth, back and forth the
robins flew with worms and bugs,
flappity-flap, flappity-flap. They
hopped around the yard to find worms,
hoppity-hop, hoppity-hop.

Every day the robins worked harder;
hoppity-hop, hoppity-hop, pulling
worms, and flappity-flap, flappity-flap,
flying to the nest. Then back to the yar
to find more worms and bugs, hoppity-
hop, hoppity-hop. Back to the nest,
flappity-flap, flappity-flap.

The little heads reaching for the
worms grew bigger and became fuzzy.
Kimberly could hear the babies' soft
peeping sounds, "Peepity-peep, peepity-
peep."

One day a cat came by and looked up at the nest. Father and Mother Robin flicked their tails, flickity-flick, flickity-flick, and screamed, "Cheat, cheat, cheat!"

In the nest the little birds' hearts beat hard with fear, thumpity-thump, thumpity-thump.

God knew why, and the robins knew why. Do you know why?

But the cat couldn't reach the nest up on the porch and went away.

Then Father and Mother Robin came back with more food and still more food. Every day the babies grew bigger. Now Kimberly saw little feathers on their heads when they bobbed up for food. Their peeping noises became cheeping sounds, "Cheepity-cheep, cheepity-cheep."

Soon the babies grew so big that the little nest was crowded. The baby birds pushed and shoved each other for more room, but there was none.

One day the babies pushed so hard that one of them fell out of the nest.

"Cheep! Cheep! Cheep!" the baby crie loudly as he fluttered down. He was so scared. But he wasn't hurt and soon hopped around the porch. Once he was out of the nest, he liked hopping and fluttering.

Very excited, Father and Mother
Robin hopped around their baby,
chirping to him, "Chirpity-chirp,
chirpity-chirp."

By the next day, all the babies had fluttered down from the nest. They hopped over the yard and even tried their wings a little. But they couldn't fl far. At night they hid in tall grass.

At first Father and Mother Robin
brought food to their babies on the
ground. Then they showed the babies
how to look for worms and bugs.
Hoppity-hop, hoppity-hop went the
babies looking for food.

Father and Mother Robin showed the babies how to sit and sleep on a tree branch all night long. They taught the babies how to sing praises to God, "Tweety-tweet-tweet, tweety-tweet-tweet."

God knew why, and the robins knew why. Do you know why?